AUTHORS

Amy Bell

Rian Bishop

Katelyn Bowles

Leona Adair

Paul Chapman

Lorena Davidson

Jack Devine

Leah Gilmour

Blake Hamilton

Ellie Hunter

Sam Kretowicz

Calvin Mackie

McKenzie McFarlane

Tyler McLellan

Josh McMillan

Summer Moore

Jack Morrison

Emma Morton

Taylor Plenderleith

Kirsten Prentice

Eve Trench

Kelice Walker

Katelynn Watt

Jak Weir

Laura Horn, Head Teacher,
Newfield Primary School
and Nursery Class

Amanda Johnston,
P6 Class Teacher,
Newfield Primary School

Introduction

'Zoe and the Magical Mindset' was written by the wonderful P6 class of 2018-2019 at Newfield Primary School, Stonehouse. The pupils were helped by advice from Mary Turner Thomson (WhiteWater Publishing Ltd) on how to create characters and develop plot.

We hope you all enjoy reading our super book as much as we enjoyed writing it. We were inspired by the P7 children from last year who created a fabulous book called 'Justin and the Magical Carrot' to create our own book. We were amazed that the children from P7 were published authors and we wanted to be the same. As the new P1 children will be our buddies, we wanted to help them overcome any worries about coming to Newfield Primary School. We would recommend this project to others as we gained many skills and enjoyed the experience of becoming published authors.

"I thought that writing this book was good fun but it was hard at times."

"I loved writing this book; I would recommend this process to others. We had to work as a team and listen to and appreciate the views of others."

"I enjoyed writing this book and would recommend it to anyone who is struggling. Remember, never give up!"

"I really enjoyed writing this book. We had to put in a lot of effort and it was tricky at times, but the feeling of accomplishment you get when it is finished makes it all worth it!"

P6 Student Comments

"We look forward to welcoming our new Primary 1 pupils to Newfield Primary at the start of every school year. It is a really exciting time for them but we also know that some pupils will be a little apprehensive and worried about starting the 'big school'.

"As part of our transition events and activities the Primary 7 pupils play an important role as Big Buddies to our new Primary 1 children. This year they have gone a step further and written a story to help reassure and welcome our new pupils. With some help and guidance from Mary Turner Thomson, the pupils have created a lovely tale of a little girl on her first day at school. I know our new pupils will love it.

"Many thanks to our P6 (soon to be P7) pupils and the class teacher Mrs Johnston for all their hard work. I am so proud of you all."

Laura Horn, Head Teacher, Newfield Primary School and Nursery Class

"I am so proud of the effort and enthusiasm shown by the P6 children in creating this book. They have all enjoyed being involved in the process of writing and illustrating this book and I hope the new P1 children enjoy reading it. It was lovely to see the children writing collaboratively and all contributing their ideas, thoughts and feelings to create such a great story."

Amanda Johnston, P6 Class Teacher, Newfield Primary School

The day Zoe had been waiting for had finally arrived. It was her first day of school. She woke up bright and early and jumped out of bed with a smile on her face. She ran down the stairs excitedly as fast as her little legs could carry her. She was delighted to smell the sweet aroma of pancakes baking in the pan.

Zoe sat down on her favourite chair at the breakfast table. Her mum walked over with two delicious fluffy pancakes and Zoe could feel her mouth watering. Her mum told her to eat up. It was getting closer to the time they would need to leave the house to walk to Newfield Primary School.

Zoe gobbled up her pancakes and zoomed up the stairs to put on her brand new school uniform. She was lucky because her mum had laid it all out on her bed neatly so all she had to do was put it on. She was very careful when she brushed her teeth so she did not stain her brand new school uniform.

Mum brushed Zoe's hair and couldn't believe how grown up she looked. Zoe grabbed her bag and double-checked everything she needed for her first day of Primary 1 was in it. She did not notice that her sparkly pink pencil case was lying on the couch under her lazy old dog ...

Mum and Zoe set off on their 5-minute walk to school. It was a walk they were used to as Zoe had gone to Newfield Nursery. On the way, Zoe smiled and waved at her best friend from Nursery, George. He looked very smart in his uniform and Zoe could see that he was super excited by the beaming smile across his face.

Before she knew it, Zoe was at the school gates. She started to feel butterflies fluttering in her tummy.

All the people in the school office welcomed Zoe and her Mum with a big smile. Zoe remembered the way to Room 1 as she had visited the classroom recently during her transition visits from Nursery. She could hear some excited chitter-chatter coming from the other classrooms in the school as she walked down the long corridor.

Finally, she reached Room 1, her new classroom.

Mrs McCafferty was standing at the classroom door waiting on her new arrivals. When Mrs McCafferty saw Zoe she reminded her to look for her peg, Zoe's peg had a picture of a brown and black cat on it. Zoe's Mum helped her to change her shoes and followed her into Room 1; her chair also had the same picture as her peg so she found it quite easily.

All the children in Room 1 were sitting in their chairs colouring in a picture of a friendly looking scruffy monster. Zoe reached into her bag for her pencil case and was shocked to discover it was not there. She began to cry and panicked a bit.

Mrs McCafferty reassured her not to worry and pointed her in the direction of the pencil tub in her group. Zoe selected a colourful rainbow pencil topped with a small brand new rubber.

Little did she know that this was no ordinary pencil ...

It seemed liked Zoe's mum had been gone for hours, however the clock on the wall only said 10am. Still ages to go thought Zoe! She continued to colour in her monster picture — Zoe loved colouring in and she felt like the pencil was encouraging her to do her best.

Mrs McCafferty clapped her hands and all of the boys and girls in Zoe's class stopped to listen to their next instruction.

It was Zoe's worst task – writing!

Oh no! Thought Zoe. I cannot do this. I am rubbish at writing. I give up!

Suddenly the friendly scruffy monster from Zoe's picture came alive, he changed his friendly appearance and was now a negative miserable monster. He said to Zoe ...

"HA HA HA Zoe, you are rubbish at writing! You will never be able to do it. Just give up and don't even try!"

Zoe felt as miserable as the monster looked but she listened to him, he was right, she was rubbish!

All of a sudden, Zoe felt something gently tapping at her shoulder. In her amazement, the colourful rainbow pencil was hovering above her. Zoe could not believe her eyes. First of all a talking monster and now a talking pencil – how much crazier could this day get?

The colourful rainbow pencil whispered softly and calmly to Zoe. It told her not to let the monster succeed. It helped her to change her mind-set and taught her to believe in herself and not give up when things get tricky. Zoe picked up the magical pencil and worked hard to do the dreaded writing task.

She started to write, it was a miracle. Zoe could not believe that with a little bit of effort, encouragement and motivation she could do anything she put her mind to!

Zoe was happily writing away when all of a sudden the magical pencil snapped like a twig into two pieces. She was devastated. The magical pencil was the only thing keeping her motivated and without it, she was lost.

The miserable negative monster was winning again. Zoe gave up.

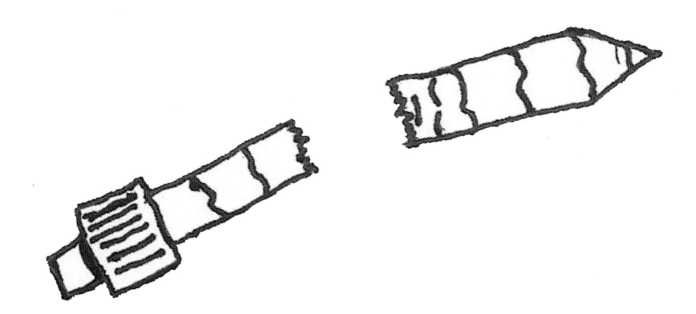

While wiping away a big fat tear from her eye, Zoe sadly looked at the pencil. She remembered how happy and proud she had felt when she had tried her best. Zoe could still hear the monster mocking her even though he was on the piece of paper.

She felt angry!

Without hesitating, Zoe grabbed the broken side of the pencil with the rubber on it and rubbed out the negative fixed mind-set monster.

She felt amazing! Why did she ever doubt herself? She finally believed in herself again and knew that if she put her mind to it she could do anything she wanted to do.

She wasn't going to let anyone put her down.

The next thing Zoe knew was that the other half of the pencil started drawing lots and lots of negative mind-set monsters.

Zoe could not believe her eyes. What was she going to do now? All these negative monsters telling her she was rubbish.

Zoe felt deflated.

Luckily, Zoe had spotted a glue stick in her group's basket. She picked up the glue-stick and carefully glued the broken magical rainbow pencil back together. This was Zoe's last hope to banish the negative mind-set monsters forever.

Once the magical rainbow pencil was back together, Zoe waited patiently for the glue to dry.

After what felt like hours, Zoe anxiously touched the magical rainbow pencil to check it was dry. The negative mind-set monsters were getting louder and more negative as the time went on.

Zoe was relieved to feel that the glue was eventually dry.

Zoe quickly used the mended magical rainbow pencil to rub out the negative mind-set monsters. Unexpectedly, the magical rainbow pencil came back to life and whispered calmly and positively to Zoe to keep going and rub away those negative thoughts.

Zoe rubbed and rubbed at the paper until the negative mind-set monsters vanished into a pile of dust. She felt proud that she had accomplished her mission. The magical rainbow pencil told Zoe to keep up her positive attitude and to always remember that if you try your best and give your best effort you will succeed.

Zoe felt that she no longer needed the magical rainbow pencil to help her and she completed her writing task with ease. She thought that perhaps someone else could maybe benefit from using it.

She glanced over at George who was having trouble with his task and looked like he was going to give up.

She knew right away what to do!

Finally, the 3 o'clock bell rang. Zoe could not believe that her first day at school was over. Mrs McCafferty walked the children to the gate and made sure that they all had someone to collect them.

Zoe was excited to see her Mum and ran over to give her a big cuddle.

Zoe tried to explain to her Mum what had happened at school with the magical rainbow pencil and the negative mind-set monsters, but Mum was having none of it.

YOU CAN DO IT WHEN YOU TRY!

BELIEVE IN YOURSELF!

NEVER GIVE UP!

ALWAYS GIVE YOUR BEST EFFORT!

YOU CAN'T SPELL IMPOSSIBLE WITHOUT POSSIBLE!

PUSH YOURSELF TO IMPROVE YOURSELF!

IF AT FIRST YOU DON'T SUCCEED TRY AGAIN!

REMEMBER IMPOSSIBLE SAYS I'M POSSIBLE!

When Zoe got home, she looked on the couch and there was her pink sparkly pencil case lying untouched. She picked up her pencil case and to her shock, the magical rainbow pencil was in her pencil case smiling back at her.